DERBLE gets a HOBBY

by: Joel Riggs

Illustrated by: Cinalyn Firando

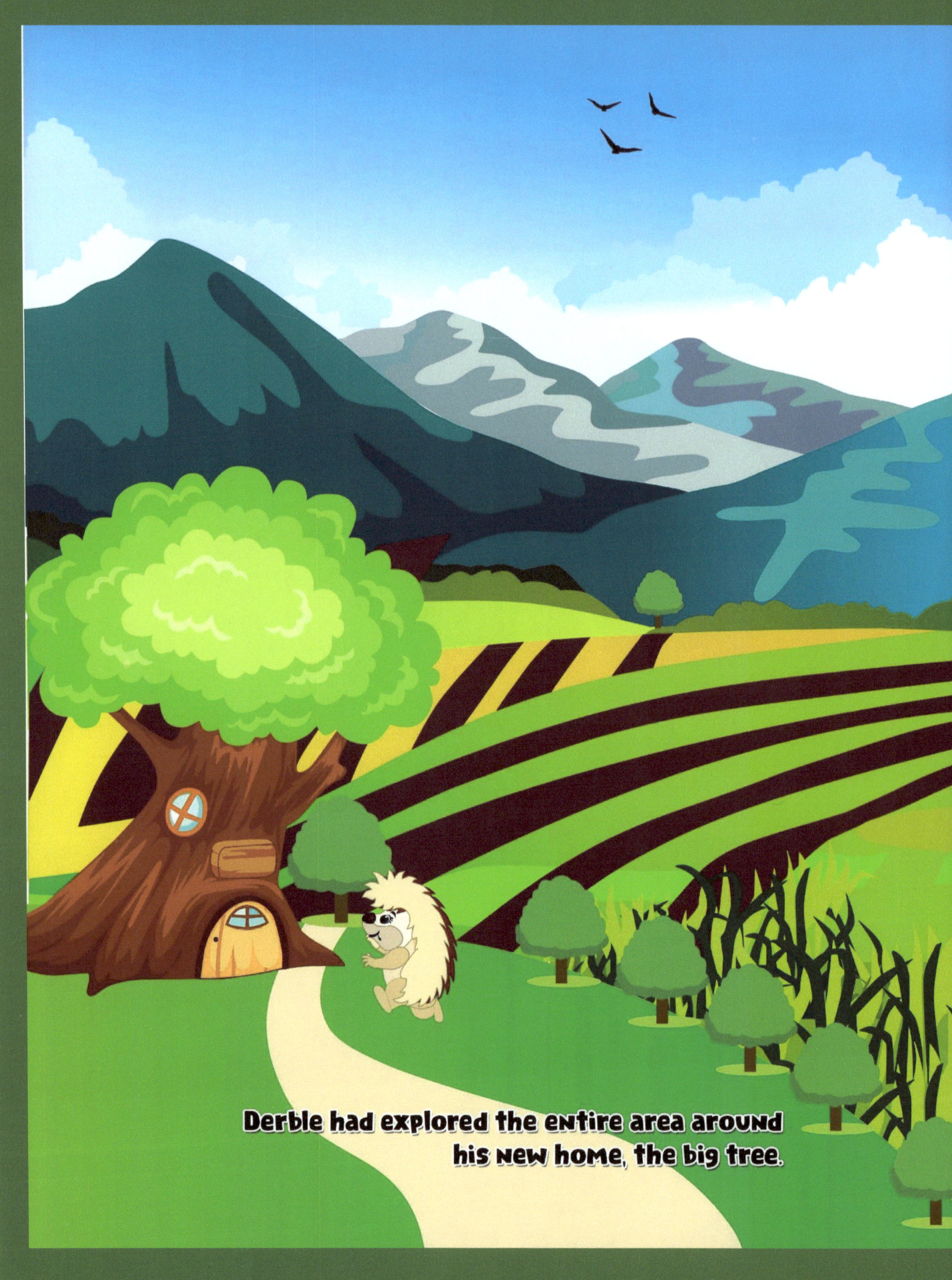

Derble had explored the entire area around
his new home, the big tree.

But yet, every time he went for a walk, he
seemed to always discover something
new about the place he called home.

So many discoveries, so many new things around him and yet he felt very comfortable there. Derble really liked his new home under the big tree.

He couldn't think of any place he liked better. Even when he was gone, visiting his cousin Jerble, Derble missed his little place.

Derble had made it really comfortable
and cozy. He had his nice warm
comfortable bed to sleep on.

He had his table and bench to Sit on,
So that he could be comfortable
when he ate.

He even had a hook, made from a root from the big tree, to hang his favorite hat on.

But for some reason, it felt like something was missing. Derble wasn't sure what it was, but he felt that same feeling every time he sat down to eat.

Derble looked around and thought
about it,but he wasn't sure what
it was. He was really happy with
his new home.

He couldn't have asked for anything better. But Something waS missing and the feelingg would not go away.

So on one particular day, when Derble
was out collecting berries,
he saw something.

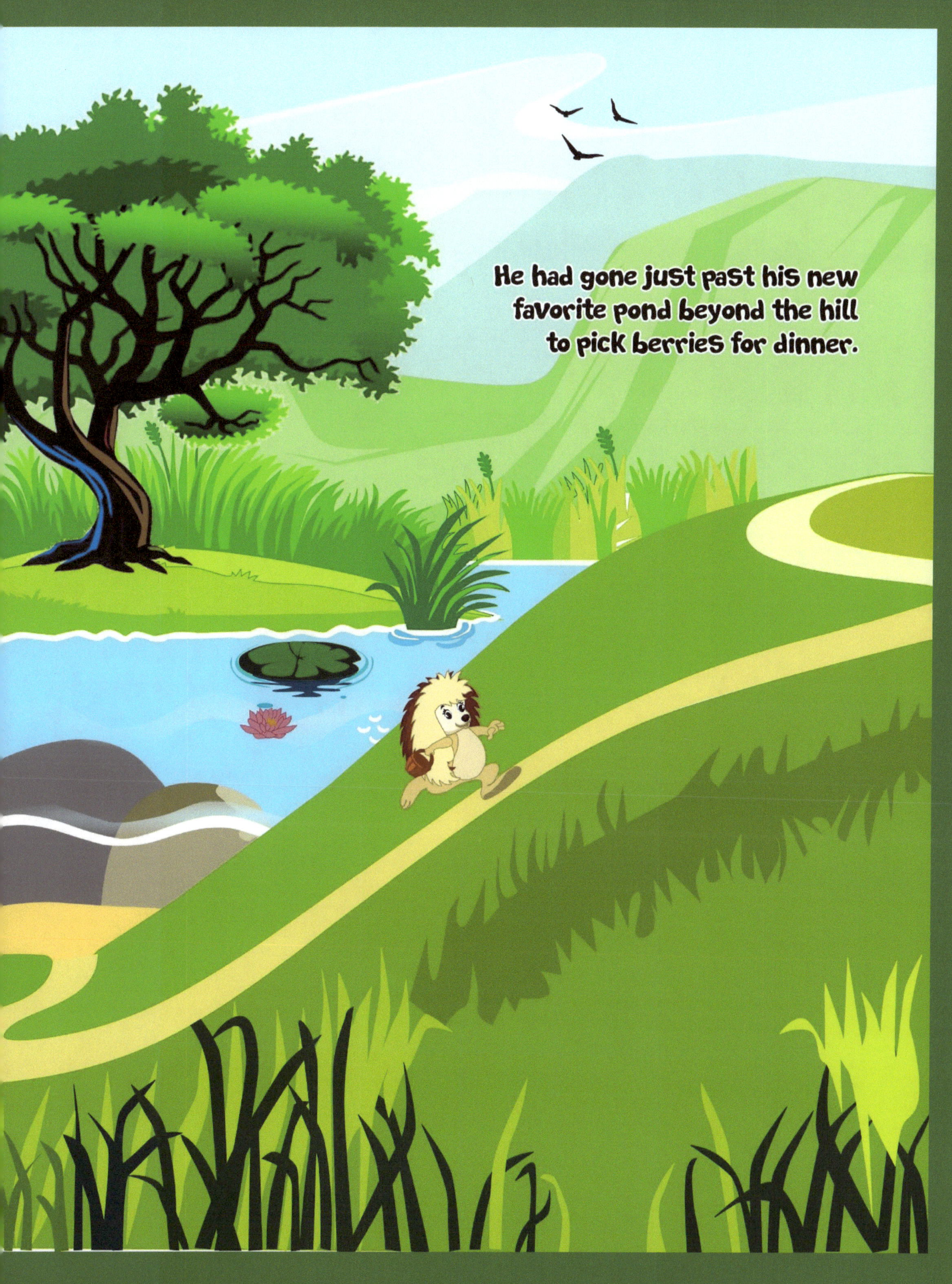
He had gone just past his new
favorite pond beyond the hill
to pick berries for dinner.

On his way back home, as he got
to the of the hill, he saw an
amazing sight

There was the big tree in the distance,
and the mountain was on the right
Side of the big tree.

The fields were different colors around the
big tree and the river flowing from
the mountain, added to the sight.

But it was the Sky that made this Sight
So Special It was this amazing blue
with clouds here and there.

It was all the different colors that came
together all at the same time that
took his breath away.

Derble stood there for the longest
time, just looking at this sight
and it came to him.

That's what was missing in his new home.
He knew right then and there that he
wanted to paint a picture of this
and hang it in his little place.

A picture to remind him how perfect his new home is and how lucky he was to find it.

Derble decided that he would even
paint one for his cousin Jerble,
and give it to him as a gift.

Derble went home and got some
supplies and he made it back
while the sky was still that
special color blue

Derble had tried painting before but
he really wanted this picture to
look like what he was Seeing

He needed to mix the colors to bring
out all of the special colors he was
Seeing. But all the extra work
would be worth it when
he was done.

Derble painted the sky on first and then he added the mountain. Next he added the big tree and then he added the fields. The different color fields made the painting come alive even more.

Derble started the next painting but
it was getting later and the sky was
blending with the setting sun

Derble didn't think that this could get any better, but each new moment brought more beauty to the evening sky.

Derble tried to capture all of this in his second picture. He was able to finish up as the sun was going down and he headed home.

He had to be extra careful not to smear his new pictures because the paint had not dried yet.

Derble hung them both up when he got home and then he went to sleep.

When he woke up in the morning, both pictures were there to remind him of the beauty that he had seen yesterday and it reminded him of how perfect his new home is and how lucky he was to find it.

And it was a good day...